Hickory, dickory, dock,

the mouse runs up the clock.

The clock strikes one.

The mouse runs down.

Hickory, dickory, dock.

Hickory, dickory, dock,
the mouse runs round the clock.

The clock strikes two.
The mouse says,

"BOO!"
Hickory, dickory, dock.